YOU ARE

KATT HEART

I0837166

YOU ARE
Words of Love, Inspiration and Healing

Katt Heart
Brea, California USA

Published by Hawks Prints Publishing LLC

Author - All Poems written by Katt Heart

Editor - Jason Smith and Linda Smith

Illustrator - Sarah Pedraja

Contributor - Cindy Kiple

April 2026

ISBN: 978-0-9992136-9-8

YOU ARE

Words of Love, Inspiration

and Healing

Author's Note

The book exists because my friends and family believed in me. Even when I could not always believe in myself. Thank you all for walking beside me, for holding space for my healing and for loving me exactly as I am...

Introduction

These poems were born in the quiet hours when love refused to stay unspoken.

They are offerings from the deepest chambers of my heart, written with gratitude for the souls who have walked beside me in this life and beyond.

The images of rivers, waves, butterflies and birds came to me as companions on the journey, symbols of a love that is both tender and untamed, deeply human and quietly spiritual.

They speak of devotion that asks for nothing in return, remembrances across lifetimes, and of the sacred presence that can be felt in a whisper of wind, or the shimmer of water.

Some of these poems are love letters, others, songs of friendship, of healing and of the invisible threads that bind us all.

In the beginning, they were written for someone specific, but they now belong to anyone who has ever loved. My hope is that as you read my poems, you'll recognize your own heart in these words, if that is to be true, then this little book has found its way home.

Acknowledgements

My heartfelt thanks to Jason Smith and Linda Smith for believing in this project and in me.

Your guidance, encouragement and generosity of spirit helped turn an idea into a beautifully designed and published book. I am deeply grateful for your support and for walking this journey beside me.

Woman of Water

Woman of water
waves embrace you...

Woman of Water

Woman of water
waves embrace you,
waves of wonder
surrounding you
with love.
Woman of water,
sail to safe harbors,
songs of
sweet harmony
with each serenade.
Woman of wonder,
Salacias riches,
arise to shine
in luminous
wisdom.
Woman of
wondrous water.

The River

The river
of destiny...

The River

The river
of destiny,
the stream
of truth,
moves thru
we two,
passing
the wisdom,
one to
another
to enlighten,
one to
another
to learn,
one to
another
to evolve,
each in
wholeness,
one to
the other.

Haiku To You

Pure light shines brightly...

Haiku To You

Pure light shines brightly,
As your radiant being,
Illuminates all...

Holding Heart

I will hold you
in my heart...

Holding Heart

When sorrow
overtakes you,
my love will
enfold you.
When the world
turns weary,
I will take your
hand.
I will hold you
in my heart,
ticking In time,
in rhythm
with your spirit,
in rhythm
with your soul.

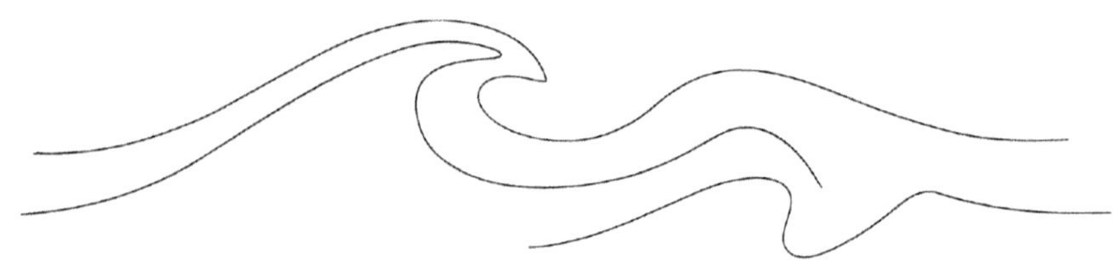

Let Us

Sometimes calm.
Sometimes roiling...

Let Us

Let us navigate
this vast ocean
of existence.
Sometimes calm.
Sometimes roiling.
Always moving,
pulsing waves,
washing over us.
Folding us under,
coming up for air,
drifting in harmony,
as the setting sun,
spills jewels
on the water.

Boundaries

To step over them
would I lose you?

Boundaries

There is so much
I want to say,
but boundaries,
hard boundaries,
bar my way.
To step over them
would I lose you?
I'd rather die
then lose you.
For life would lose
It's meaning.
Life would lose its joy.
So I'll stay on my side
and wish you well.
Up on the edge,
of the boundary,
I dwell.

To Kauai

Fragrance fills the air,
the perfume of living...

To Kauai

Fragrance fills the air,
the perfume of living.
Gaia abounds,
surrounding us
in scent,
surrounding us
with sentience.
Infusing us
in wonder.
This is what
the spirit
sings...
Gaia smiles.

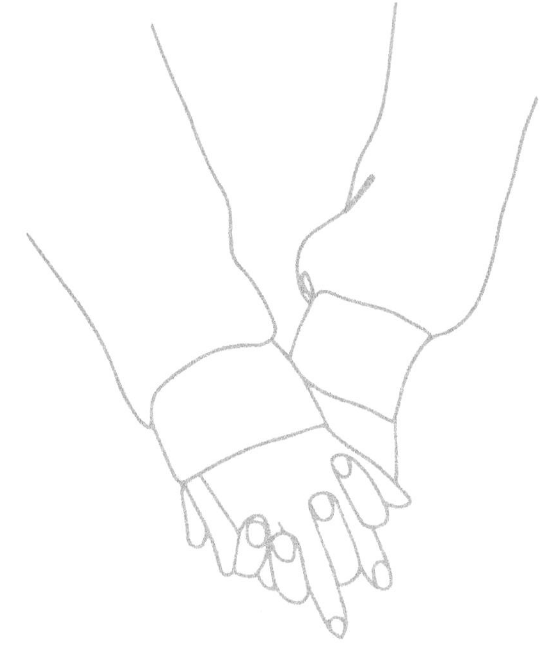

Lively, Lovely, Friendship

Let us keep our lively,
lovely, friendship...

Lively, Lovely, Friendship

Let us keep our lively,
lovely, friendship.
You don't have to know
how deep
my feelings go.
Although I know
that you do know
and keep it closely.
If you ask me to be honest
I will truthfully tell you,
that I love you
beyond words,
beyond understanding,
beyond all rhyme or reason,
beyond time or measure,
to the depth and breath
of my being.
So please, don't ask me.
Let us keep our lively,
lovely, friendship.

Spirits Of The Air

They glide
over calm waters...

Spirits Of The Air

May the spirits of the air,
guide and protect you,
today and every day.
They are messengers,
from the great stream
of consciousness,
they are of the heart,
love, empathy,
and compassion.
And of the mind,
wisdom.
They glide
over calm waters.

I Stand With You

I stand with you
always
and forever...

I Stand With You

I stand with you
my love
I stand with you
always
and forever.
Je suis avec toi
Mon amour,
Je suis avec toi
toujours et
pour toujours.

On Cat's Paws

On cat's paws
I shall amble...

On Cat's Paws

On cat's paws
I shall amble,
quietly,
thru it all.
On cat's paws,
direct and registering,
not at all poetic,
but accurate.
Slinking,
free stealing,
softly,
circling,
purring.
Perching
with delight,
in quiet
contemplation,
and quiet
contentment.

Butterfly

My love rests peacefully,
as darkness descends...

Butterfly

My love for you
is a butterfly,
dancing amongst
the sweetest flowers..
My love rests peacefully,
as darkness descends,
awaiting
the quiet moment,
at dawning
of day.
My love is of spirit
transcending
this mortal coil.
My love is
Forever, forever
and always.

You Always Saw

You always saw
the spark...

You Always Saw

You always saw
the spark.
You've ignited
the flame.
Not a fire
of destruction,
but a fire
of creation.
You are
adored
beyond
the boundaries
of this
existence.
Let radiance
light every corner
of the darkness,
let the spirit
permeate
your world, with love.

Waves

Waves flowing outward...

Waves

Waves flowing outward.
Ever expanding circles.
Perceptions alter.

To Tiger Baby

The protocol
of being
a cat...

To Tiger Baby

Kitten,
so new
to
the world
and yet
he knows
perfectly well,
the protocol
of being
a cat.

Ireland's Song

Ireland calls me home...

Ireland's Song

Ireland calls me home,
an ache of remembrance.
The Aes Sidhe are dancing,
in the green woods,
singing...
Bigi linn.
(Come join us!)

Aes Sidhe - the people of the mound, (fairies).

My Love

My Love for you
is beyond love...

My Love

My Love for you
is beyond love,
in a place deep
and unknowable.
It is pure
and selfless.
It seeks
only your
happiness and
well being.
It seeks to
surround you
in light.
You have
my heart,
I give you
my devotion.
Always and forever,
my devotion.

Bird Of Paradise

To catch your eye,
to win your love...

Bird Of Paradise

I shall
unfold
my
finest
feathers
for you.
I shall clear
a sacred space
and dance.
To catch your eye,
to win your love,
A Bird of Paradise.

In Your Quiet Way

You have healed
my grieving heart...

In Your Quiet Way

In your quiet way,
you have
loved me.
With words
Unspoken.
You have healed
my grieving heart,
in your
quiet way.
And found
the touch
to mend
all
that
was
broken.
In your
kind and
deeply moving
quiet way.

In The Garden

The forgotten self
remembers...

In The Garden

In the garden
of being,
we have
remembered.
Timeless,
ageless,
ancient fire
shining thru
the darkness.
Reaching out
in reflection.
The forgotten self
remembers.
Evolving
to fulfillment.
The river
of destiny
moves thru us,
forming waves
upon the water.

I Think Of You

I think of you
as the wind...

I Think Of You

I think of you
as the wind,
gently
whispers.
As waves
softly sing to
the welcoming
shore.
I think of you...
I think of you
as the moon
shines
so brightly,
serenading
the
twilight,
with
the sweetest
refrain,
I think of you.

A Soothing Balm

Would
that I could
heal...

A Soothing Balm

Would
that I could
heal
the deepest
wounds
that life
has left
upon thee.
I fear
they reach
far too deep,
too numerous,
to find.
And thus
I offer
what I can.
A soothing balm
of never
ending
love.

I Journey

I journey
with you...

I Journey

I journey
with you
to weave
the threads
that tie us,
one to all.
The universal,
unwavering call,
weaves quietly,
to embrace
the whole.
Wrapped in
wonder
steeped
in awe,
forever
awake,
in bountiful
celebration.

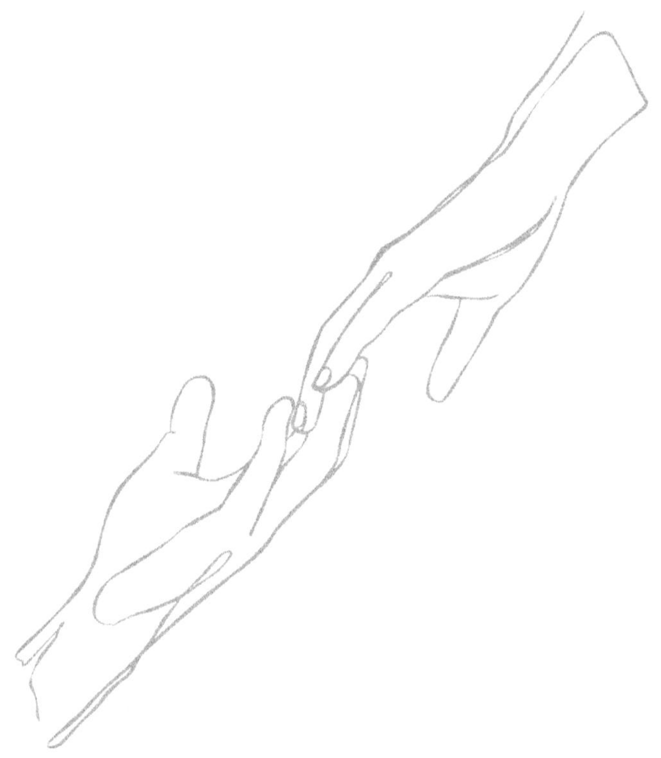

Finally

I've found
you...

Finally

Finally
I've found
you.
I've searched
for
so long,
centuries
it seems,
searching
a
loncly
way.
Searching
for
a hint,
a whisper,
of you.

A *Muse*

A muse
is smiling...

A *Muse*

A muse
is smiling,
brighter
than
the waking sun.
She knows,
that she
has lit
the dawn,
with her
radiance.

The Greeks

This is love beyond love,
love beyond expectation...

The Greeks

The Greeks
cannot define
my love for you.
Philia or Philo?
Agape won't do.
This is love beyond love,
love beyond expectation,
or understanding.
I could presume you
to be my twin flame,
or split apart,
or most truly
my soul mate.
But it is not
for me to say.
It is only for me
to love you
with all my heart
and soul. With all,
my bounteous
spirit.

What Is This Madness?

I know, I know, I lied to you...

What Is This Madness?

What is this madness
that has descended upon me?
What is it that makes
my heart flutter
and my body swoon?
I know, I know, I lied to you,
thinking that my feelings
could stay hidden.
But you know
and I know, that you know,
though no words
were ever spoken.
The arrow of Eros.
is straight and true,
it is a madness,
that has no cure,
a sweet madness,
of joy and sorrow.
A madness
only time will
soften.

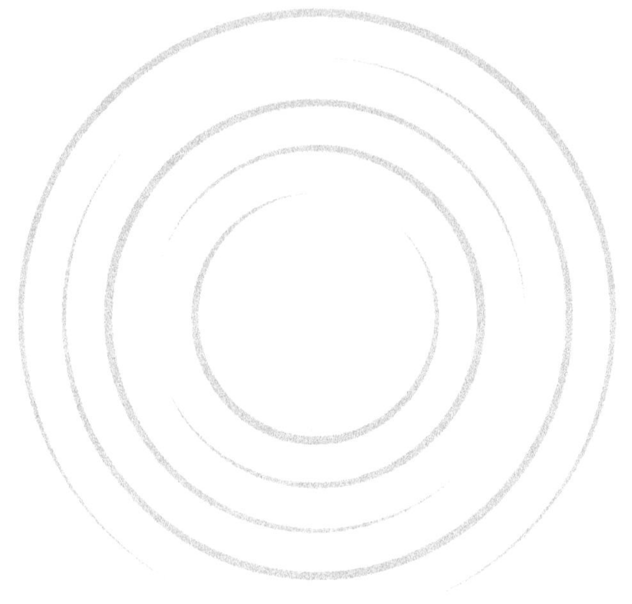

True As You

Ripples
on a
pond...

True As You

Ripples
on a
pond.
Emanating
outward.
Ever
outward.
Altering
the nature
of what
seems
to be
real,
to what
is true.
True
as you,
my love,
true
as you are...

Ripples...

Waves of love
ever forward...

Ripples...

Waves of love
emanate outward,
enfolding others,
in an infinite
embrace.
Waves of love
ever forward.
In view of you,
I have become Love.

The Heart Of Marron Rouge

I see your words
across the miles...

The Heart Of Marron Rouge

I see your words
across the miles
and a heart
of Marron Rouge
in your farewell,
and I forget,
I forget,
my senses.
I'm dreaming.
Yes, I trust you, words,
precious words,
and a heart
of Marron Rouge
that sends
me reeling
and
lights
my
very
soul.

My Love

My love for you
is as light as air...

My Love

My love for you
is as light as air.
A soft whisper.
Etherial,
delicate,
divine.
Beyond
the cruel
reaches
of this
perilous world...
In a place
that will
always be...

The Sacred

The sacred
surrounds us...

The Sacred

The sacred
surrounds us,
singing
it's
own
special
song.
A melody
of wisdom,
on waves
of sound.
Singular
resonance,
dance
and swirl.
Guiding
us
thru
this revel
of being.

Quantum Love

It is as infinite
as the starry sky...

Quantum Love

I cannot contain
my love for you.
It is as infinite
as the starry sky.
And as singular
as the
smallest grain
of sand.
It is as deep
as the ocean
And as tiny
as a teardrop
in the rain.

Greta Oto

Beloved,
You are as rare
and gracious...

Greta Oto

Beloved,
you are as rare
and gracious
as the glass
winged butterfly,
scattering sunlight
into rainbows
as you
arabesque
thru the air.
You, who
were unseen
for so long,
as darkness
descended.
Until sunlight
shown again
and lit
your lovely
elegance.

I Shall Dance

I shall dance
in celebration of you...

I Shall Dance

Je dancerai
dans un champ de lilas
tandis que
un cerf blanc
attend en repose
I shall dance
in a field of lilacs,
while the white stag
waits in repose.
I shall dance
in celebration of you,
of your being
in the world...
In a field
of lilac flowers,
while the white stag
guides my quest,
my spiritual journey,
with you, in a
sacred place
of being...

May All Your Tears

May all
your tears
wash away...

May All Your Tears

May all
your tears
wash away.
May the past
be folded
into time.
There is only
always and
forever,
there
will
always be...
butterflies,
dragonflies,
and
hummingbirds,
beloved.

The Blessing Of...You

The essence of you,
fills me with wonder...

The Blessing Of…You

The sacred
sensed my sorrow,
saw my tears
stain the darkness,
and brought me
the blessing of you.
The blessing of you,
the bounty of your love.
The blessing of you,
your radiant brilliance.
The essence of you,
fills me with wonder.
My heart overflows,
with…
The
Blessing
Of
You…

Time Is The River

So many centuries of searching,
to find you now...

Time Is The River

I could not hold on
all those centuries ago
and you were lost forever,
or so it seemed...
So many centuries of searching,
to find you now.
This is my redemption.
Next time, precious one.
Next time.
Now, you are,
forever found.

No Need To Ask

The answer
is simple...

No Need To Ask

No need
to ask me
why
my love
is so
selfless.
The answer
is simple.
I'm standing
in the stream.
Je sais
que tu
comprends?

I Sought You Out

Consciousness
in painful recognition...

I Sought You Out

I sought you out
for consciousness,
pure selfless
consciousness
in painful recognition,
being born anew,
in wisdom
and understanding,
in spiritual knowing,
in spiritual awakening.
Was I selfish
in doing so?

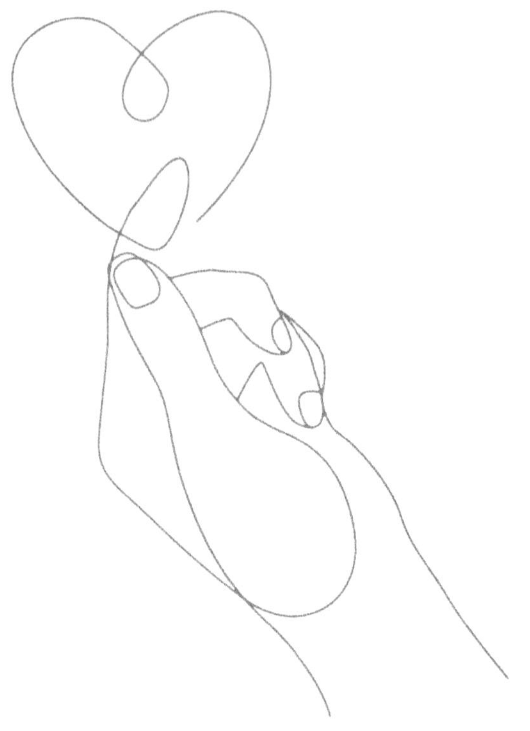

Beyond Love

I love you
beyond love...

Beyond Love

I love you
beyond love,
beyond reason,
in a place
I've never known
and
always longed for.
In a place
I never dreamed
that I would find you,
in a place,
that fills my heart,
to overflowing.

Ripples

Ripples on a pond.
A butterfly...

Ripples

Ripples on a pond.
A butterfly
flutters it's wings.
An imperceptible
alteration
in the
unfolding flower.

Inner One

Inner One
weep no more...

Inner One

Inner One
weep no more,
I'll lift you
from deep waters.
Wounded one,
I'll heal you.
My sacred love
will free you,
to fly from
depths
of despair.
A bright,
new day,
is dawning.
A love
that has
no boundaries,
infinite,
unfolding with light.
bountiful, beautiful,
being...

Therapists Would Say

I say,
that it is,
my redemption...

Therapists Would Say

Therapists would say,
that loving you,
so selflessly,
is not in
my best interest.
I say,
that it is,
my redemption.

Missing Piece

My bitter
heart
to gold...

Missing Piece

Your love has
held
a missing
piece
of the
puzzle
that is
truly
me.
A portion
that turned
my bitter
heart
to gold.

How Could I?

How could
I ever
not love you?

How Could I?

How could
I ever
not love you?
How could
I never
feel you
with me?
You light
every instant
of my being,
in joyful
celebration!

You Have

You have inspired
a steady stream...

You Have

You have inspired
a steady stream
of consciousness
in me,
that flows,
ever outward,
to an open sea,
and flowing further
to the ocean,
of consciousness...
Consciousness,
that roils
in me.

Is It All

Is it all
a lesson in futility?

Is It All

Is it all
a lesson in futility?
Is it all
a hopeless quest?
To hold a love,
that cannot be?
To love
in all futility?
What am I left with?
A soul on fire,
the primordial fire
of creation.
Just knowing
that You
are in the world,
fills my spirit
with inspiration.
No futility
reborn,
in fire and light.

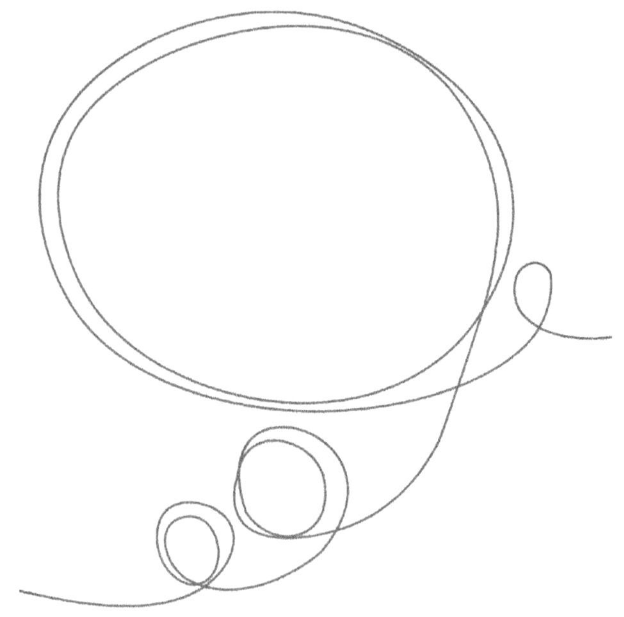

Some Words

There are some words
that I hold sacred...

Some Words

There are some words
that I hold sacred
in the deep
recesses
of my
trembling heart.
Were you
to see them,
my fear
would
overcome me,
my fear
that you
would say
No More...

Elemental You

You,
elemental
You...

Elemental You

You are the fire
that lights
my inspiration,
the water
that sustains me.
You are the air
that lifts my spirit,
and the earth,
that holds
me placed.
You are,
you are,
you are,
You,
elemental
You...

A Stream Is Singing

A Stream is singing,
emanating outward...

A Stream Is Singing

A Stream is singing,
emanating outward.
A Vessel fills,
flowing
into
this world,
endless,
artesian,
clear &
blessed
waters.
Spirits sing
a song
of
sweet
awakening.

You Are

www.ingramcontent.com/pod-product-compliance
Lightning Source LLC
LaVergne TN
LVHW011030110826
845149LV00015B/3365